THE X FILES™
COLLECTION

STEFAN PETRUCHA

CHARLES ADLARD

TOPPS COMICS
NEW YORK

CONTENTS

An Interview with Chris Carter

"Not To Be Opened Until X-Mas"
Originally presented in THE X-FILES #1

"The Dismemberance of Things Past"
Originally presented in THE X-FILES #2

"A Little Dream Of Me"
Originally presented in THE X-FILES #3

"Firebird Part One: Khobka's Lament"
Originally presented in THE X-FILES #4

"Firebird Part Two: Crescit Eundo"
Originally presented in THE X-FILES #5

"Firebird Part Three: A Brief Authority"
Originally presented in THE X-FILES #6

"Trick Of The Light"
Originally presented in THE X-FILES Hero Illustrated Special

Artists' Profiles

THE X-FILES™ created by Chris Carter

Stefan Petrucha
writer

Charles Adlard
artist

John Workman
letterer

George Freeman & Laurie E. Smith
colorists

Digital Chameleon
separations

Jim Salicrup
Dwight Jon Zimmerman
editors

THE X-FILES™ COLLECTION Volume 1, Number 1, July 1995. Published by TOPPS COMICS INC., One Whitehall Street, New York, NY 10004-2109. THE X-FILES is TM and © 1995 Twentieth Century Fox Film Corporation. All Rights Reserved. The story, characters, and incidents mentioned in this magazine unless otherwise noted, are entirely fictional. MARS ATTACKS is a registered trademark of The Topps Company, Inc., and used with permission. DOOM II is a trademark of id Software and used with permission. Topps Comics, Inc., is a wholly-owned subsidiary of The Topps Company, Inc. **ISBN #1-883313-07-4** First Printing. Printed in Canada.

AN INTERVIEW WITH CHRIS CARTER

Conducted by Dwight Jon Zimmerman

What is your impression of THE X-FILES comic book stories?

I like them very much. I love the cover art. It's interesting because they are different than what I do but they are an interesting addition to The X-Files--it's interesting to see someone else's take on The X-Files stories.

What was your intitial feeling when you saw your creation interpreted in another medium?

My initial feeling was that I had created a monster. [Laughter]

How so?

Well, you never anticipate that something that you do, characters that you create will take on lives of their own. And in these comic books, they've taken on lives past my parental supervision. And that's a curious thing. It's like seeing your kids go out there and try and make it in the world.

You still oversee what goes on in the comics and have input.

Yes. I get sent the comics. I get sent the cover art and I nod my head "yes" or "no." Usually I nod my head "yes." But beyond that I do see thumbnail story treatments and I really look for an area rather than any kind of serious execution in those things. So really I've depended upon the good taste and the talent of the people involved in the comic books to protect the integrity of The X-Files and to perpetuate the spirit of The X-Files.

Do you think the comic book series has been successful in that?

I think so. I think the success of the comic book series is a direct indicator of that.

What does the crew think of the comic?

They love them. They can't get them fast enough. It's funny. Sometimes I've actually seen crew members with comic books before I have them.

Ooooo. We'll have to fix that. How about the cast's impression?

The cast loves them. I think that Gillian loves them more than David. I think that he's not so hot on the way his character, his caricature, looks. [Laughter]

We're working on that.

But I think it's interesting, actually, I think it's an artist's interpretation, so it works fine for me.

Do you feel the comic has been effective in capturing the mood of the television series?

Yeah, I think so. I think that everyone working on the comic understands the dark mood of THE X-FILES both in story tone and in the look of the show. I think that the look of the comic is rather cinematic in the choices of the panels--although I notice that Frohike has a lot more hair than he really does. [Laughter]

Do you find that you prefer oneshots or multi-parters?

As far as comic book stories go, it's funny, I actually don't have an opinion on that. I like what works. And so far I think that the comic books have really worked for me. I'm actually looking forward to the upcoming three-part series that you are working on. I'm looking forward to seeing how that plays out, because I know how hard it is to do two-parters or three-parters on the show. They each have to function independently and together. So it's a real trick. Of course, comic book readers can easily refer back to the previous comic book. When you're doing a television show if someone didn't capture it on tape, they don't have that luxury.

We are fixing Scully's blond hair in the second issue's story so that it's less blond in this edition.

Well, we do change her hair sometimes. So you have to stay on top of what we're doing as well.

Very true. Would you like to write an X-FILES comic book story?

I'd love to try writing one when I have the time.

When you're ready, give us a call. We'll do everything we can to make it happen.

Great, I'd love to do that.

What can you let fans know about what they can expect in the third season?

The third season is more scary stories, and answering the questions we posed in the second season's finale, "Anasazi." After that as far as I'm concerned, it's "X-Files Forever."

THE TRUTH IS OUT THERE

"LUCIA DOS SANTOS, AGE NINE, FRANCISCO MARTO, EIGHT, AND HIS SISTER JACINTA, SIX, ALL FROM PORTUGAL.

"IN SPRING, 1916, IN A FIELD CALLED CHOUSA VELHA, THEY BEGAN HAVING VISITATIONS-- FIRST FROM A RADIANT MAN, THEN A LUMINESCENT LADY.

"THE VISITS CONTINUED. BELIEVERS GATHERED, HOPING TO SEE THE VIRGIN MARY. THEY WEREN'T DISAPPOINTED.

"JUNE 13, 1917, THERE WERE FIFTY PEOPLE. JULY 13, FIVE THOUSAND. SEPTEMBER 13, THIRTY THOUSAND.

"ON OCTOBER 13, FIFTY TO EIGHTY THOUSAND PEOPLE AT THE SITE SAW A 'SMOKY, SILVERY DISC' MANEUVER IN THE SKY.

"MANY BELIEVED IT WAS THE SUN-- MOVING. EVERYONE BELIEVED IT WAS A MIRACLE."

I'VE MISSED YOUR SLIDE SHOWS, MULDER. IT'S NICE TO SEE YOU SO EXCITED.

BUT WHAT MAKES THIS AN X-FILE? WE ARE STILL PART OF THE FBI. HAS THE BVM BEEN SPOTTED IN WASHINGTON?

I WAS HOPING THE PHRASE "SILVERY DISC" MIGHT GIVE IT AWAY, SCULLY.

BUT IF YOU'D KINDLY RETURN YOUR GAZE TO THE SCREEN-- THERE'S MUCH MORE.

THE LADY GAVE THE CHILDREN A SERIES OF PROPHECIES.

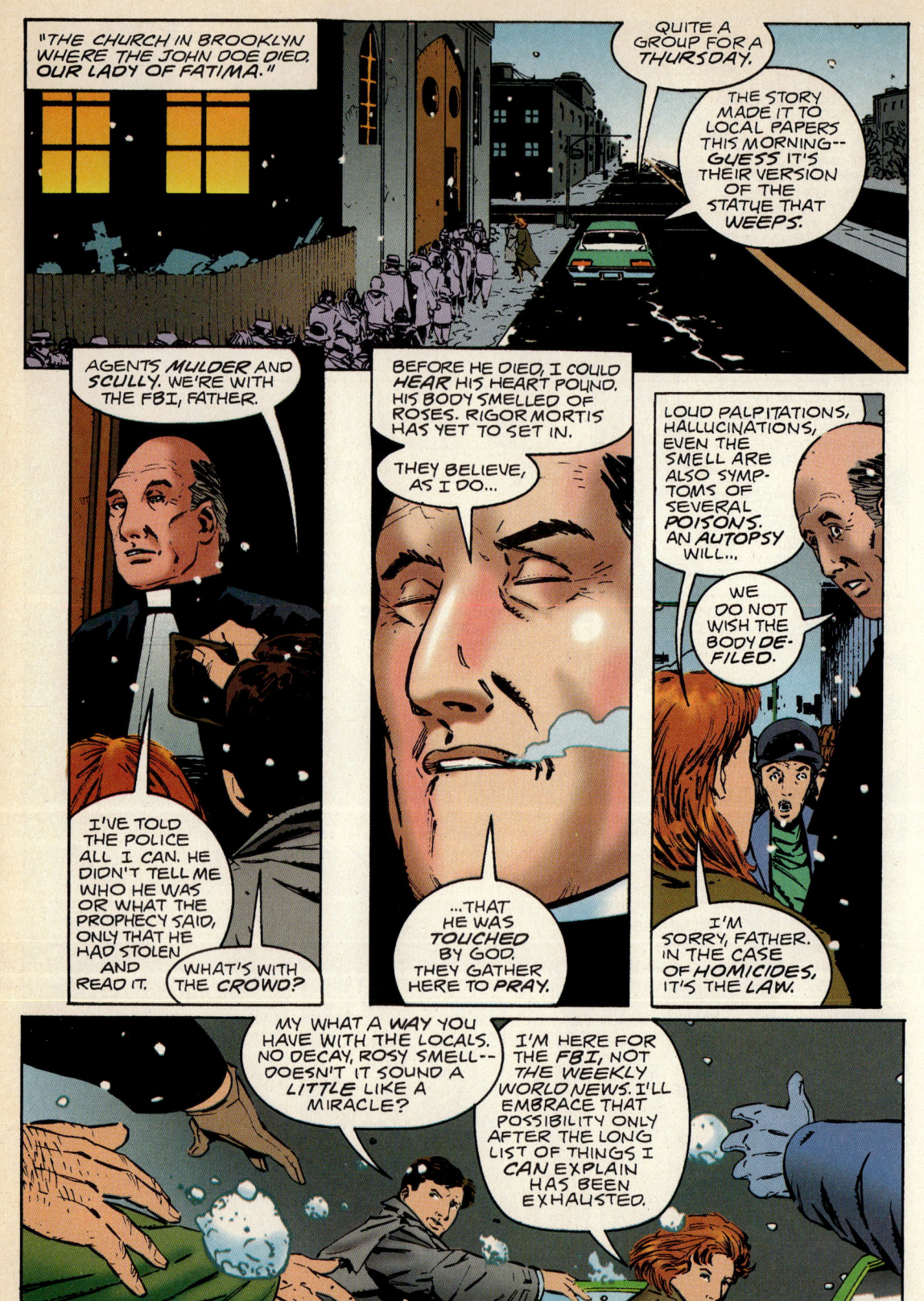

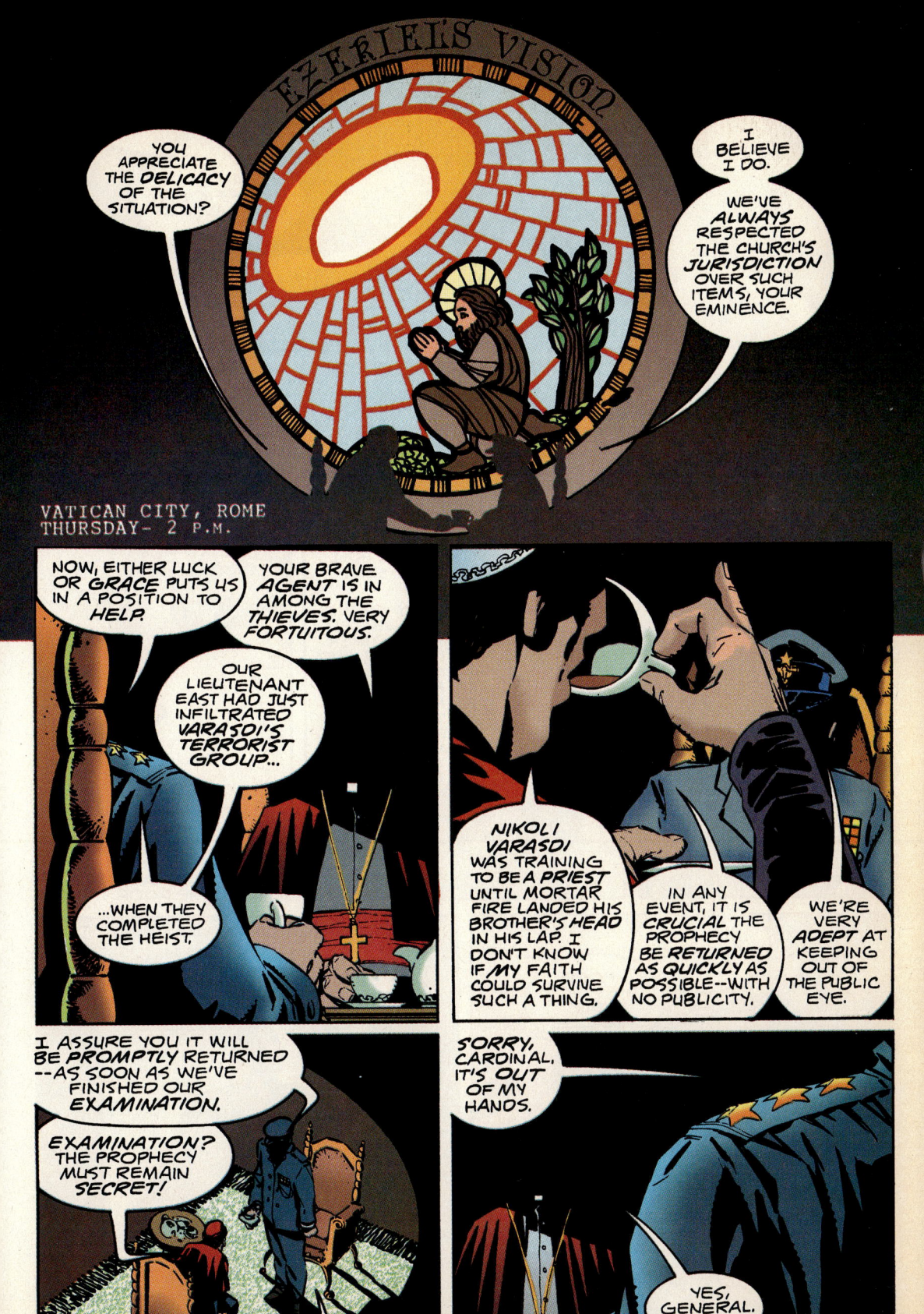

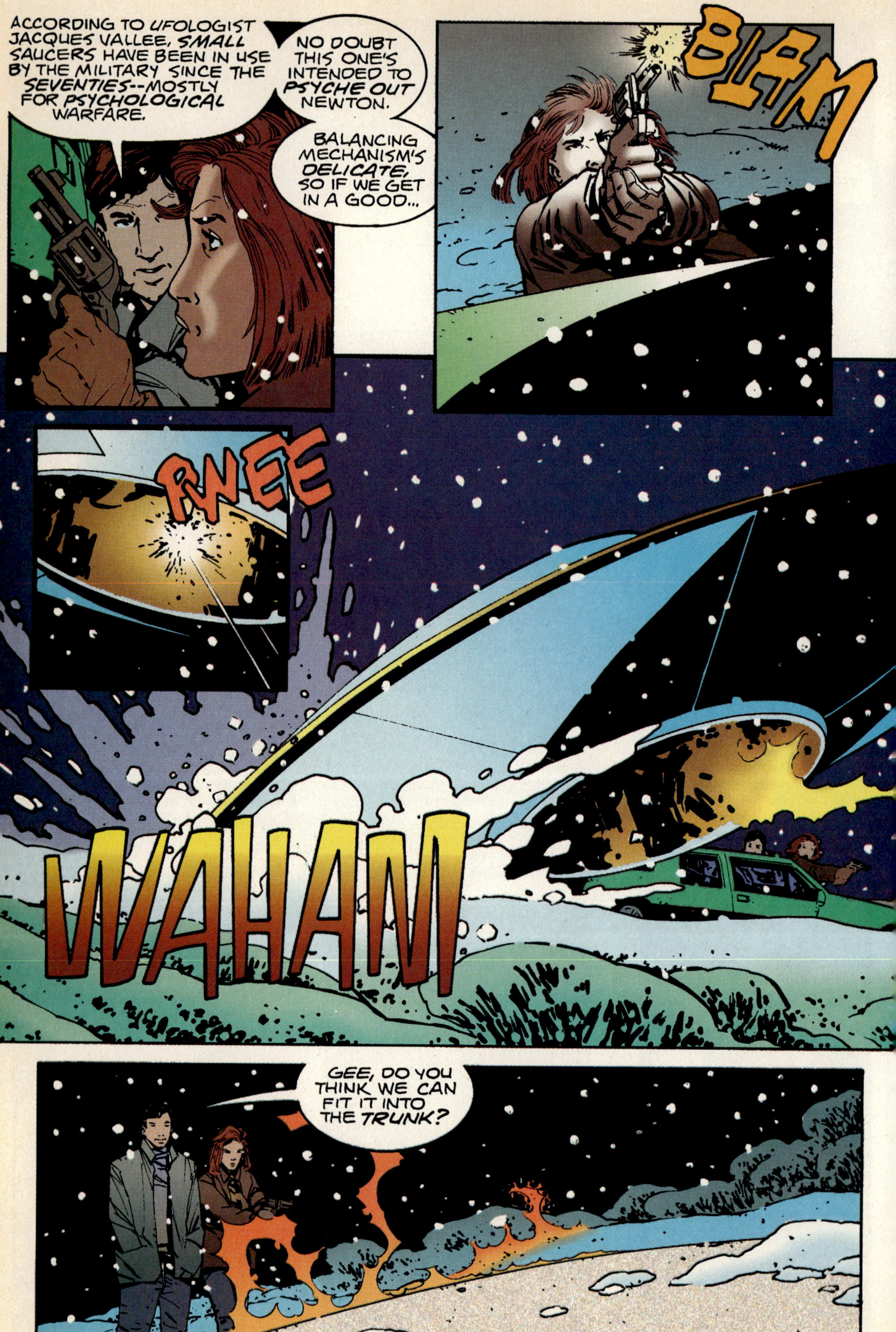

NEOLA, KANSAS
THE EDWARDS HOME
6 A.M.

MMMM

I REMEMBER.

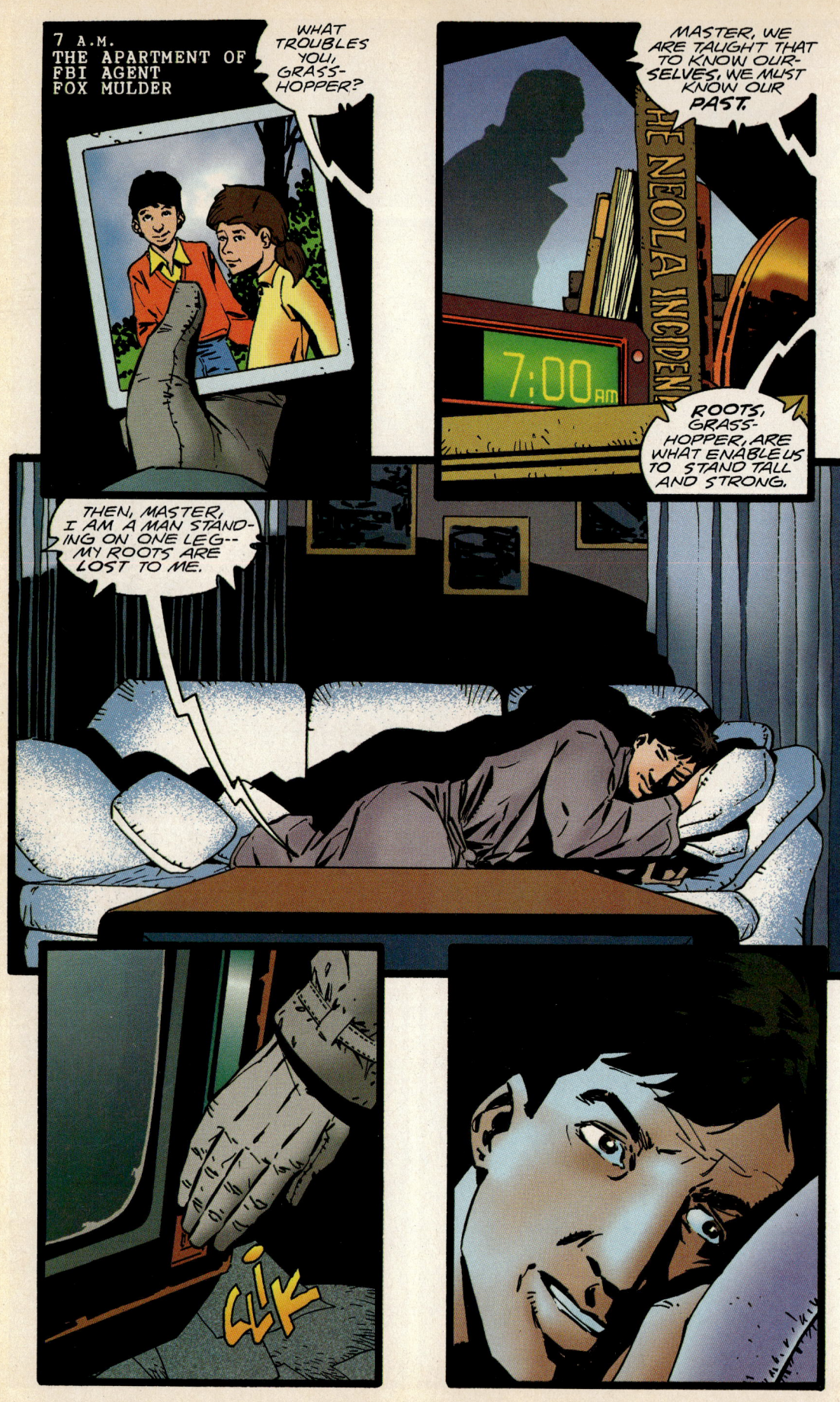

"AT BEST, I CAN TRY TO CONJURE IT FOR YOU WITH WORDS, TRY TO MAKE YOU FEEL JUST A LITTLE BIT OF WHAT I FELT.

"BUT I CAN'T PUT IT IN YOUR HANDS AND SAY, 'HERE, HERE IT IS--TOUCH IT... JUST TOUCH IT... AND YOU'LL KNOW'.'

"IS WHAT I REMEMBER REAL?"

"IN THE END, I DON'T CARE.

"THAT'S A QUESTION I CAN'T ANSWER. AFTER ALL, MAYBE I'M CRAZY. MAYBE I'VE BEEN LIVING IN A DREAM ALL THESE YEARS.

"FOR ME, IT DOESN'T MATTER IF IT'S REAL THE WAY A DESK OR A PHONE NUMBER IS-- BECAUSE EVEN IF IT'S FAKE, IT'S MORE.

"AND YOU KNOW I CAN'T COUNT IT BECAUSE I CAN'T COUNT THAT HIGH AND I CAN'T WEIGH IT BECAUSE THERE ARE NO SCALES THAT WORK THAT WAY.

"I JUST HAVE TO REACH, WHEN I CAN, WITH WHATEVER I CAN... AND TRY TO TOUCH IT.

"IF THERE IS SUCH A THING AS TRUTH OUT THERE, THAT'S THE ONLY PLACE I'VE FOUND IT."

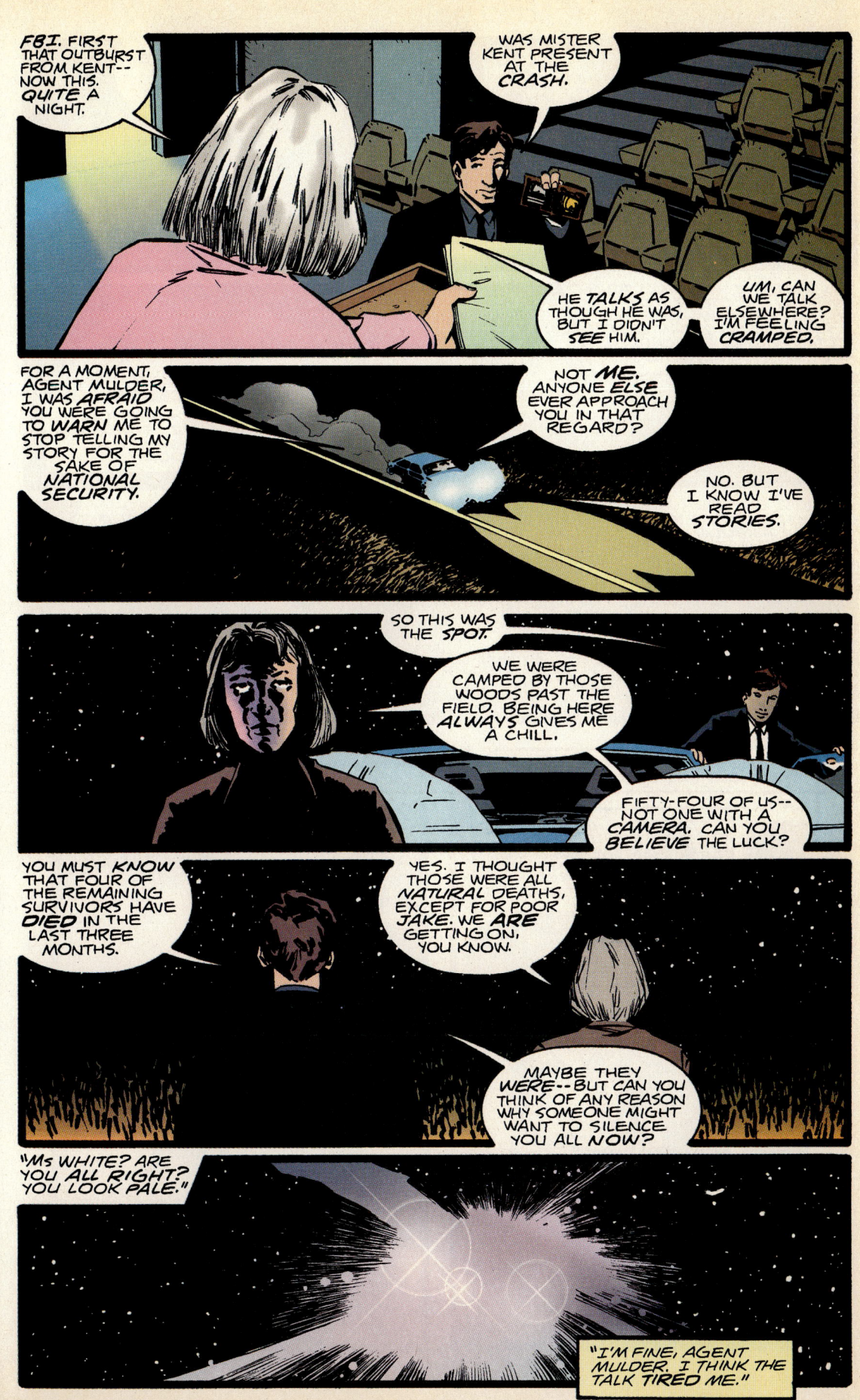

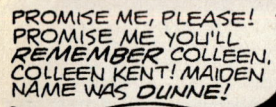

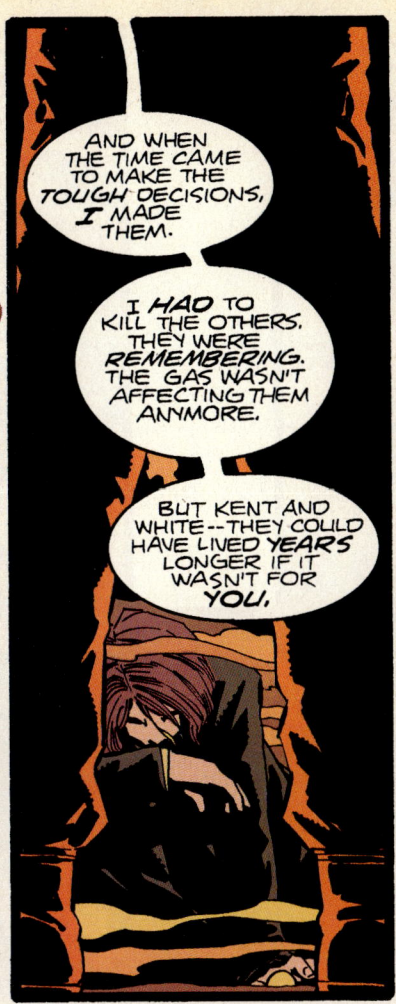

"Who among us wants to believe that our grasp on reality is so _provisional_, that reality in fact is impenetrable and unfathomable because it is _only what we remember_, and what we remember is rarely the literal _truth_?"

**"THE MYTH OF REPRESSED MEMORY"
BY DR. ELIZABETH LOFTUS
& KATHERINE KETCHAM**

TO BE CONTINUED

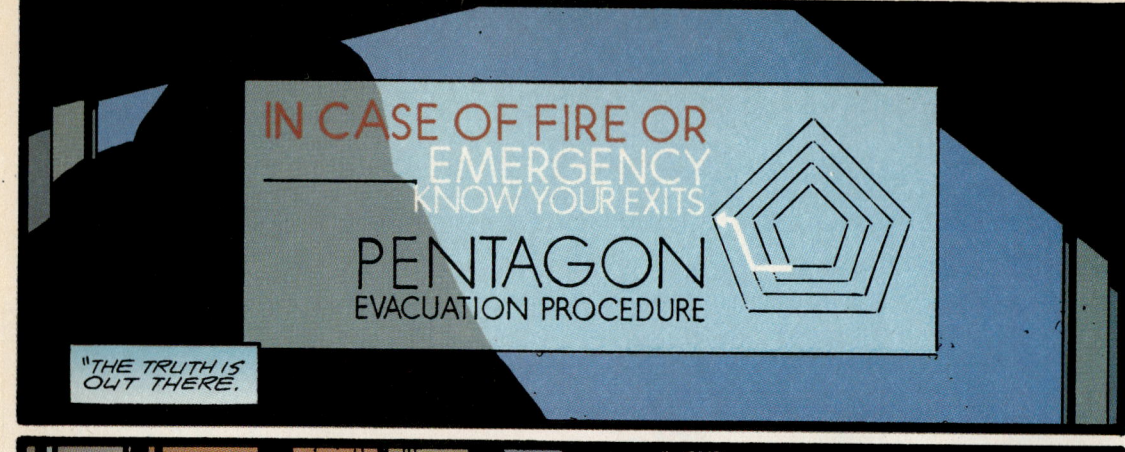

"THE TRUTH IS OUT THERE."

"BUT THERE'S ANOTHER TRUTH IN HERE."

"A TRUTH THAT VANISHES LIKE A DROP OF MILK SUSPENDED IN WATER--WHENEVER YOU TRY TO TOUCH IT."

"MY NAME IS MULDER. I'M AN AGENT FOR THE FBI, A TOOL OF THE LAW... OCCASIONALLY A TOOL OF JUSTICE."

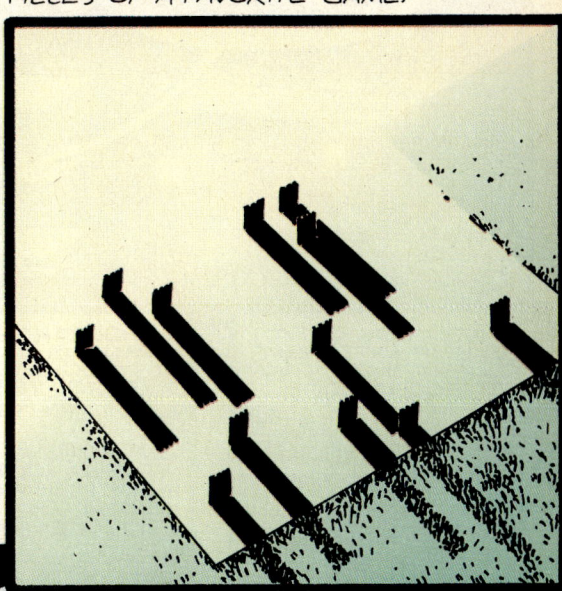

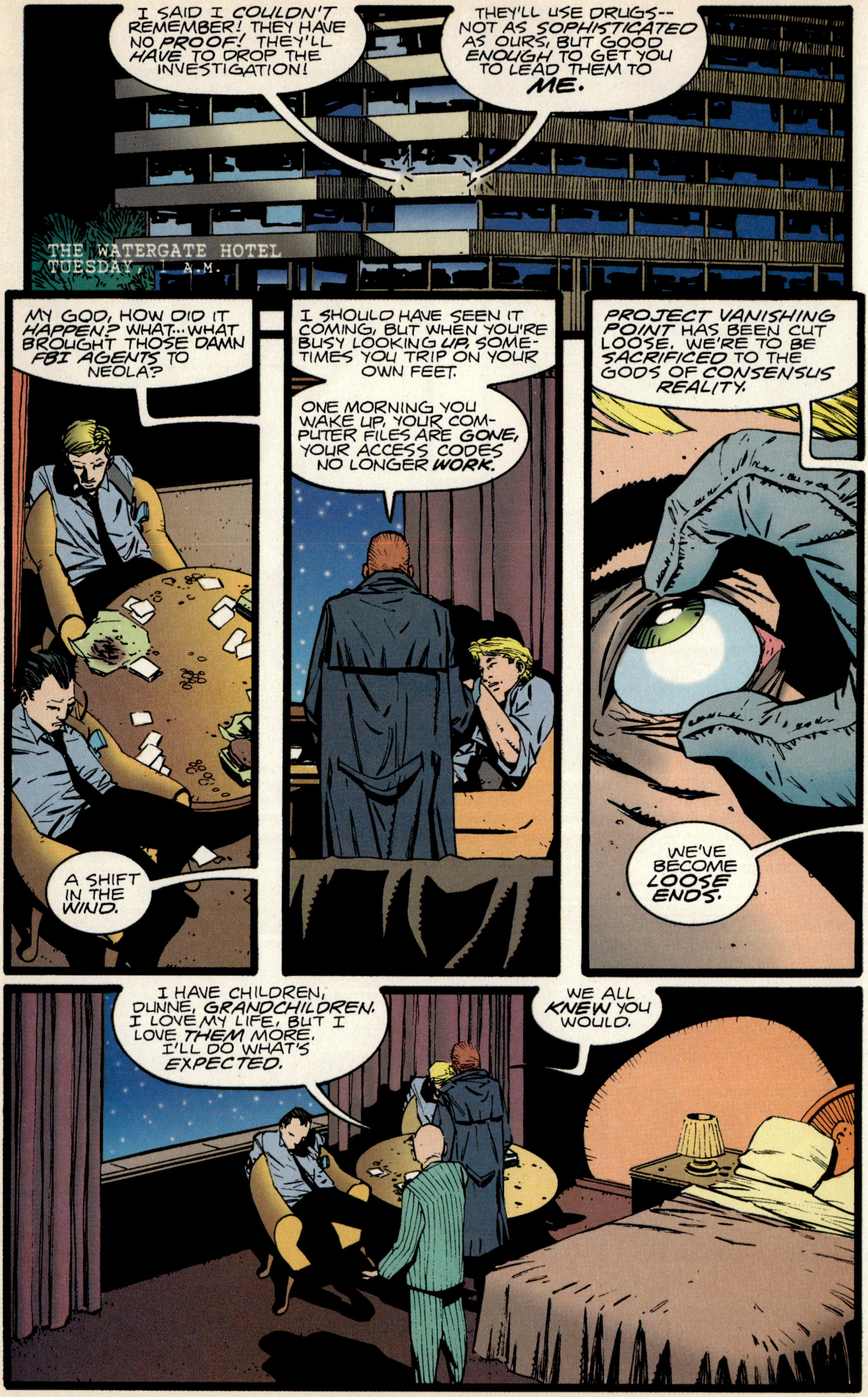

Austin O'Malley once wrote, "Memory is a crazy woman that HOARDS colored RAGS and throws away food". Right now, I'd be happy with EITHER.

I suffer MEMORY gaps. Agent Mulder, his insomnia quelled by medication, is having horrific NIGHTMARES.

Had we also been subjected to the appropriate BRAIN-WASHING techniques, our entire experience of the past might have been completely RE-WRITTEN.

The gas we were exposed to is still under analysis. Early results indicate it affects the NEURO-LINGUISTIC areas of the brain.

The heart-attack DEATH of General Palmer put an early end to the Senate investigation of the Neola incident.

Mulder believes he was part of a dark "INNER GOVERNMENT." While I'm dubious as to the extent of such a group, the possibili—

RING

"MOM! Thanks for the forget-me-nots. I'm just fine... a little LIGHT-HEADED. They say we're going to be RELEASED tomorrow."

"How's DADDY?"

BETHESDA NAVAL HOSPITAL
THURSDAY, 11 A.M.

"My poor darling-- don't you REMEMBER?"

"He's been DEAD for almost a year."

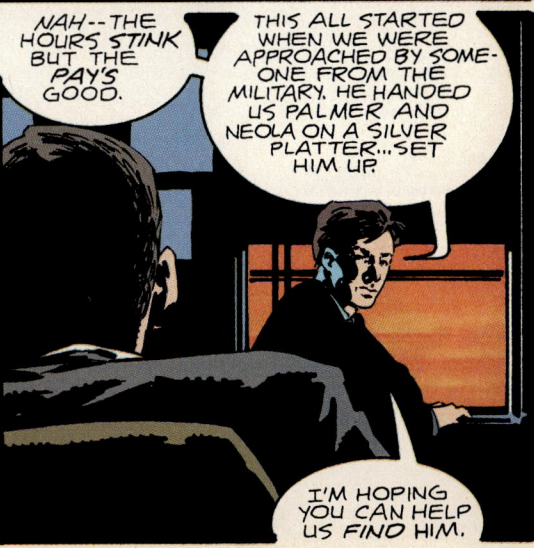

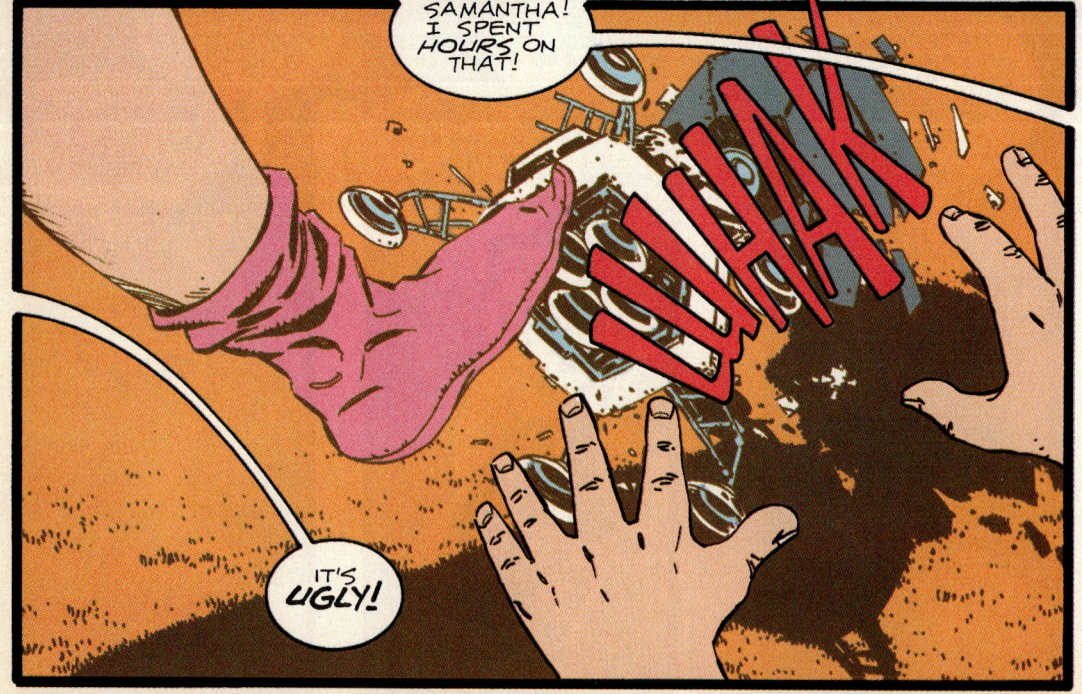

JUNE 6, 1908
TUNGUSKA, SIBERIA
EARLY MORNING, EXACT TIME UNKNOWN

SINCE YOU CAME, FIREBIRD, SO ANGRY FROM THE SKY
TO TAKE REVENGE ON THE BLACK EARTH
FOR HER ADULTERY WITH THE MOON

MY HEART HAS BEEN A WIDOW

FROM THAT TIME ON, I WAS NO LONGER THE SHAMAN'S SON
HUNGRY ONLY FOR HIS FATHER'S MAGIC
SINCE THEN NO ONE, NOT EVEN MY BROTHER THE FOX

CAN SPEAK MY NAME

I HAVE BECOME THE EARTH YOU RIPPED APART THE SKY YOU CUT AND LEFT BLEEDING

AS HELPLESS AS THE FOREST

YOU SHREDDED INTO RAIN.

BUT THE SKY CLEARS AND THE EARTH GROWS FERTILE. WHY THEN, FIREBIRD, ARE YOU STILL BOUND? WHY DO I REMAIN, A KEEPSAKE OF YOUR RAGE? IS THIS SAD HABIT WHAT IT IS TO BE A GOD?

FIREBIRD Part One
KHOBKA'S LAMENT

TUNGUSKA, SIBERIA
NOVEMBER 24, 1994
8:47 A.M.

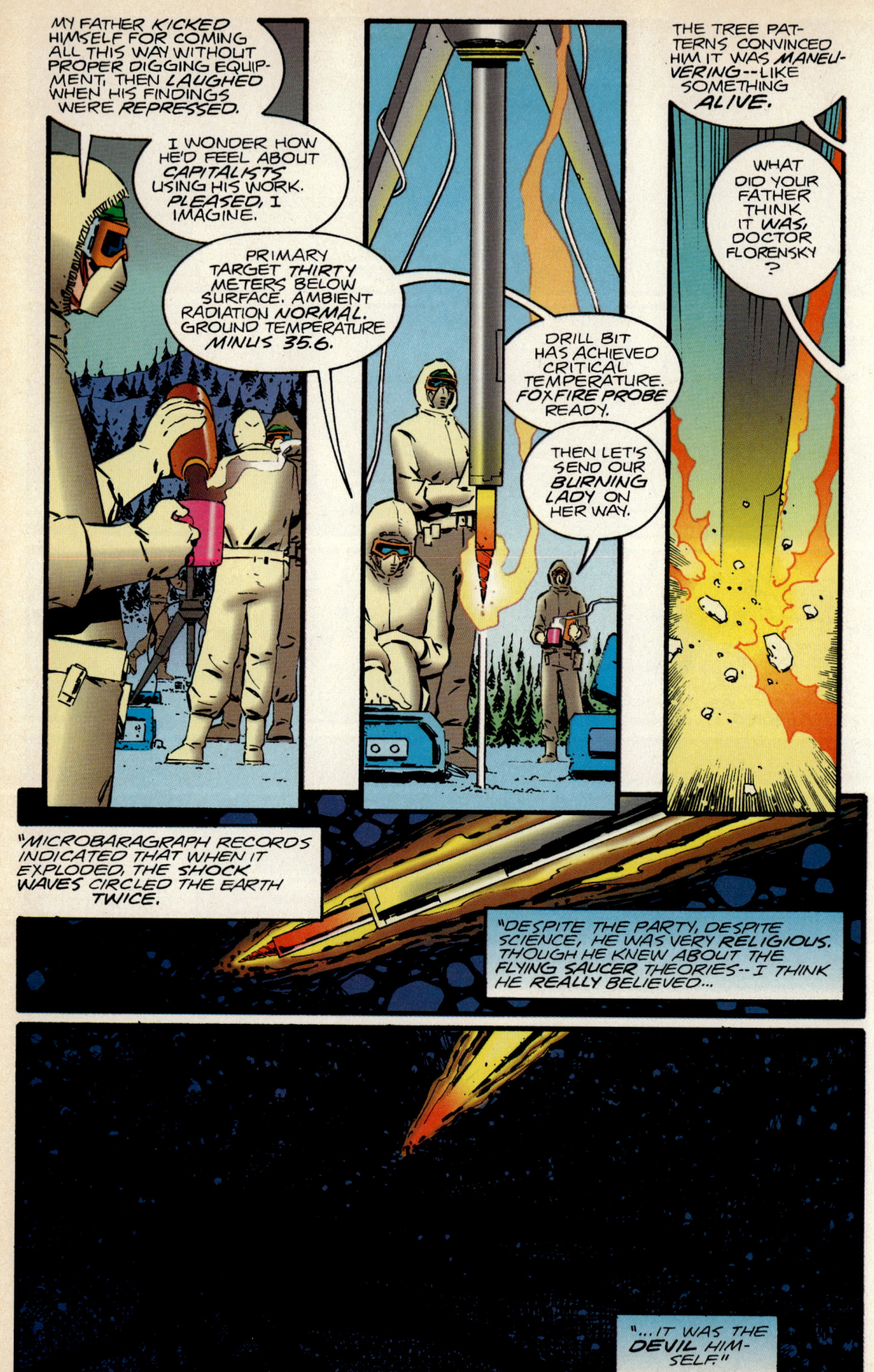

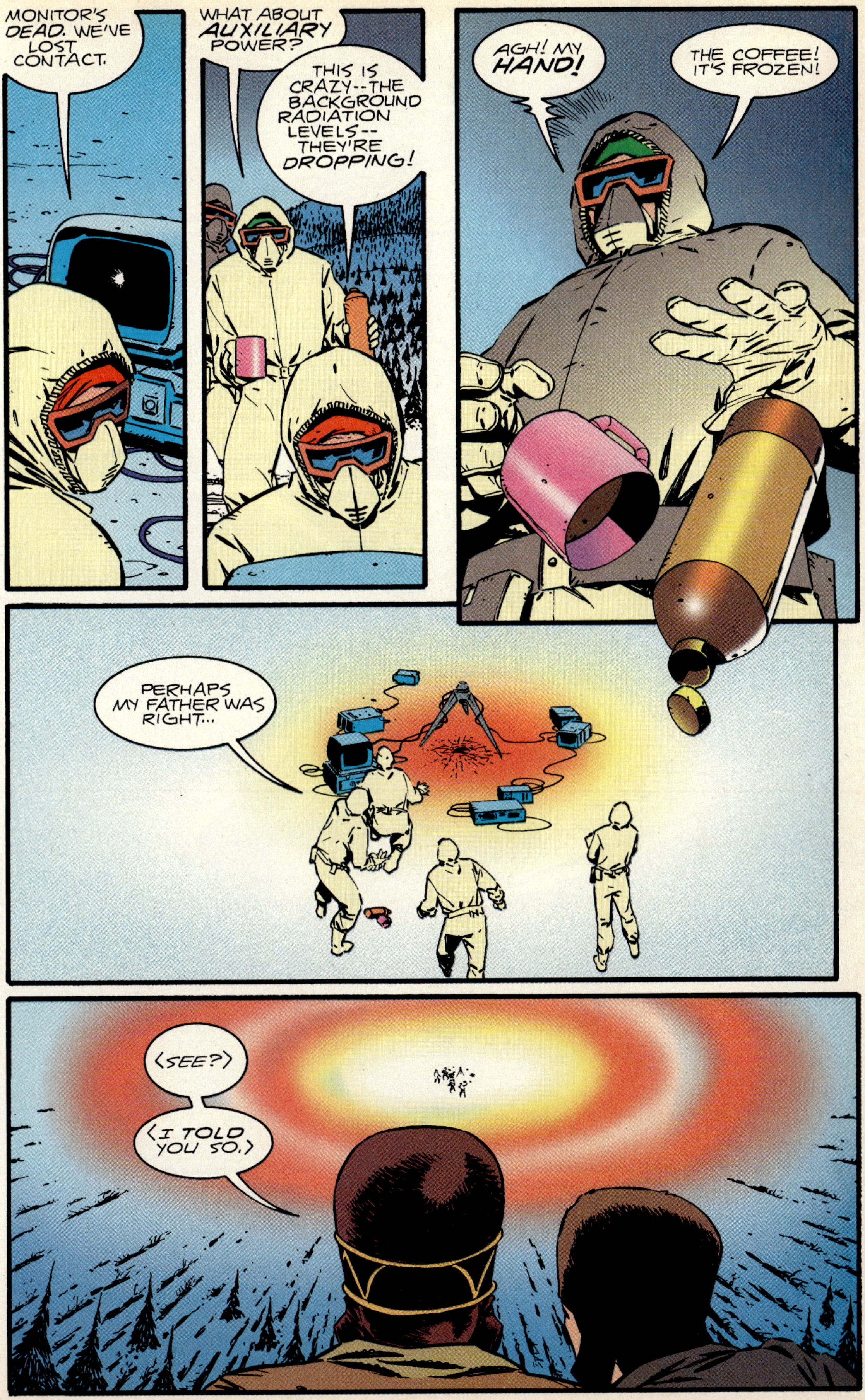

US 70
ALAMOGORDO, NEW MEXICO
APRIL 1, 1995, 3 P.M.

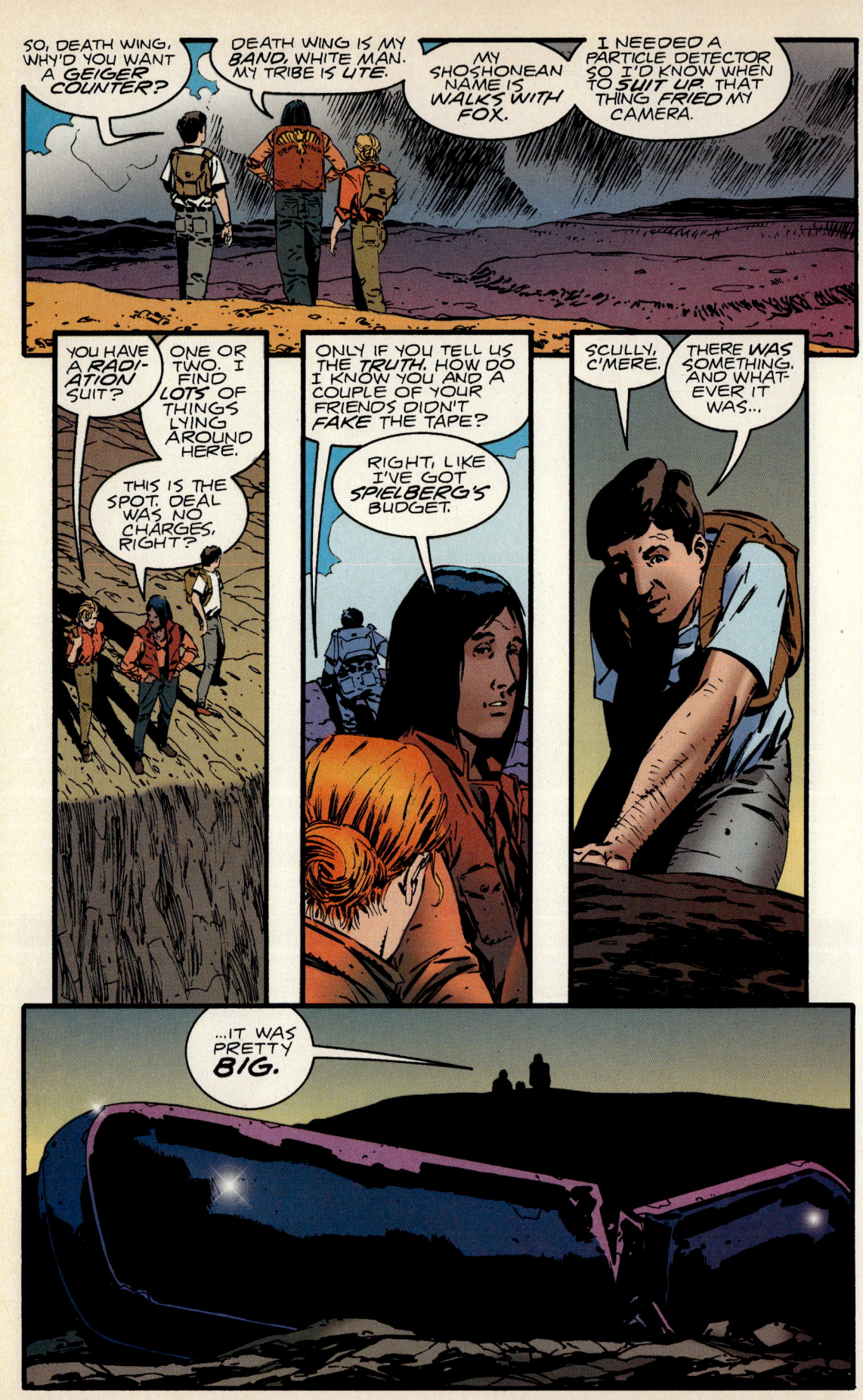

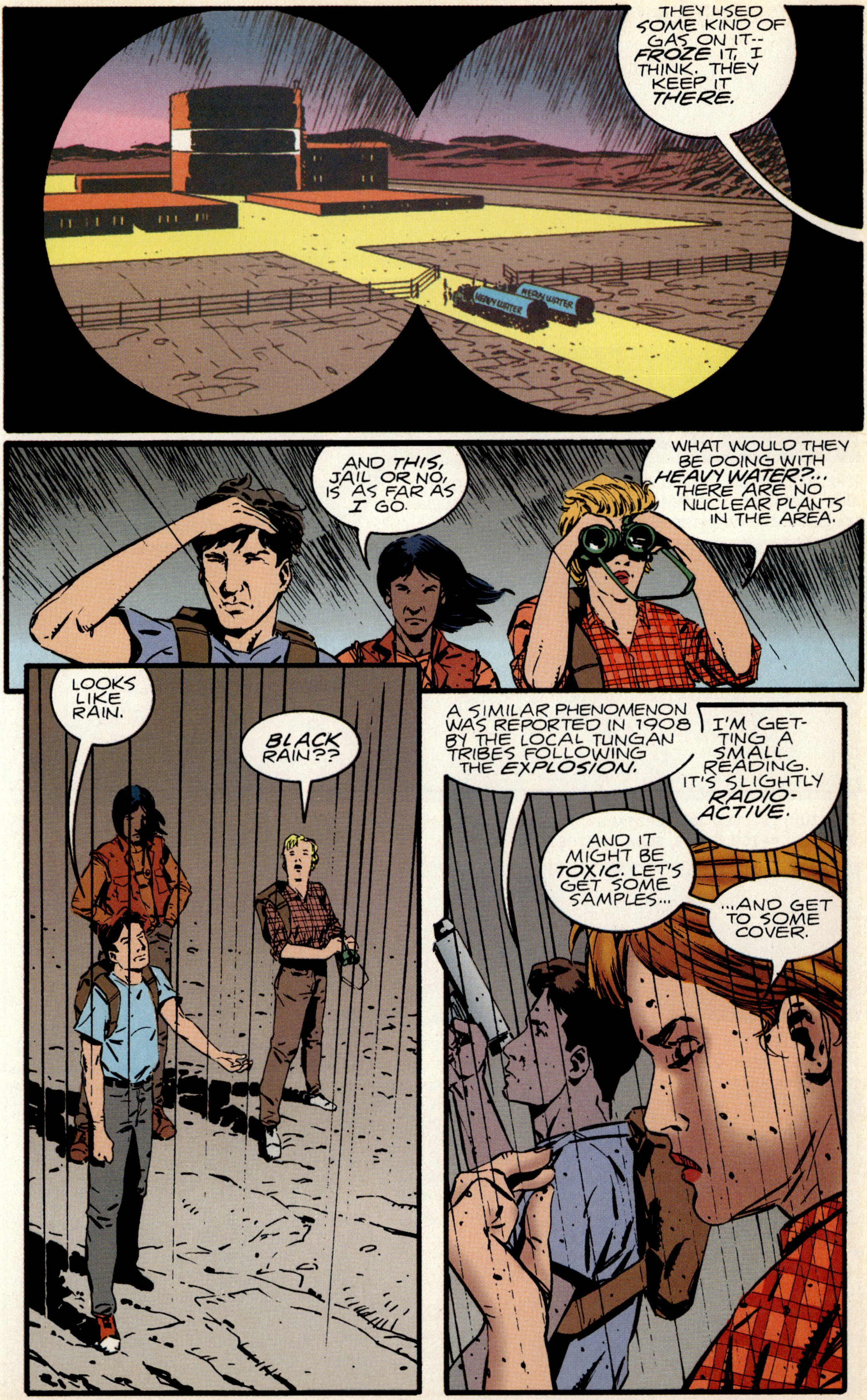

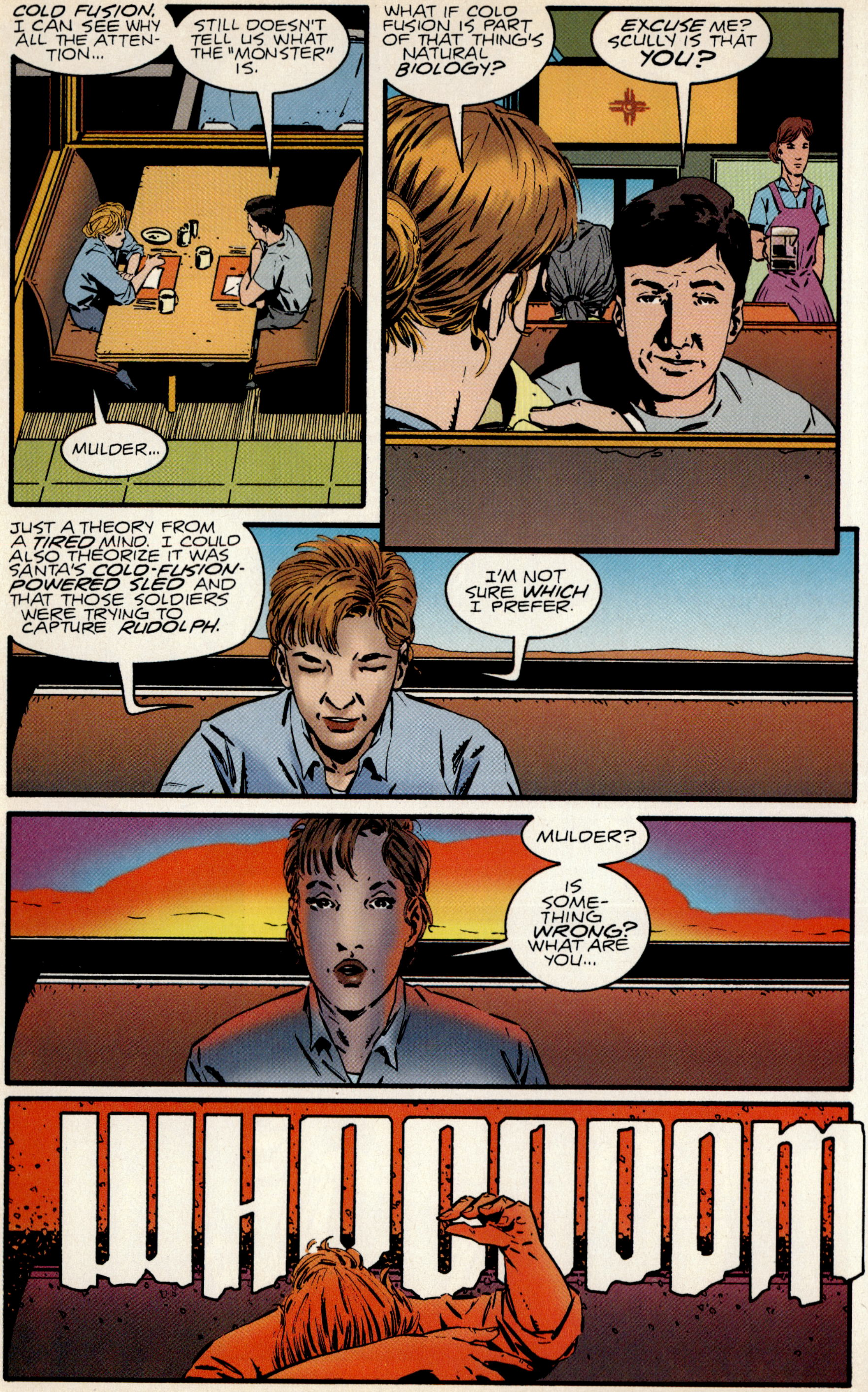

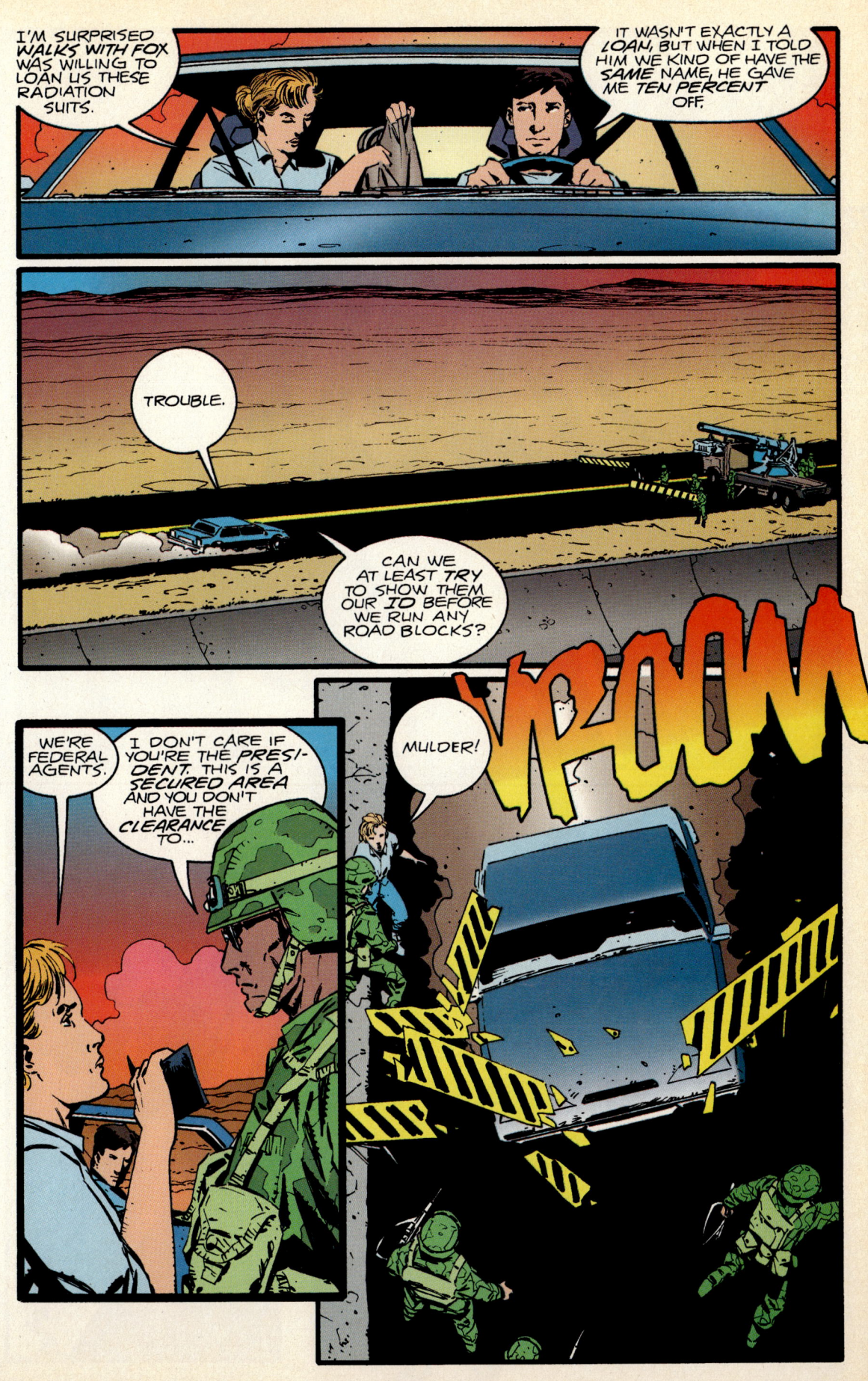

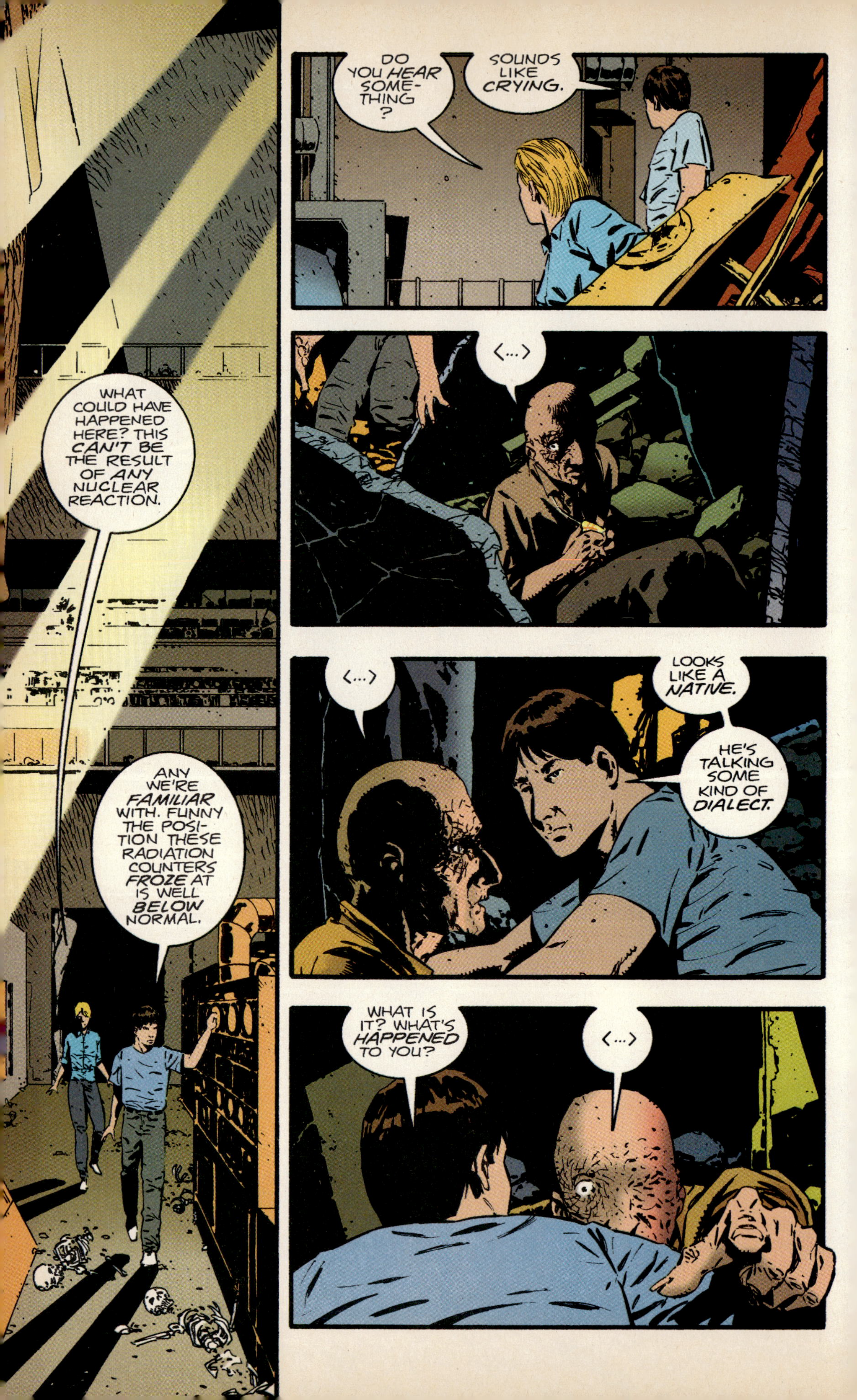

"NOT A GOOD TIME TO DRAG YOUR FEET!"

"MULDER, WHAT *IS* THAT THING?"

"WELL, EITHER IT'S A *DEEP SPACE* ENTITY WITH *COLD FUSION* BIOLOGY THAT TOOK A WRONG TURN AT *TUNGUSKA* IN 1908."

RIPPP

"OR THE LOST EPISODES OF *JACQUES COSTEAU* ARE LOTS MORE *EXCITING* THAN ANYONE GUESSED."

"WE'VE GOT TO GET TO A *HOSPITAL*. WE'VE PROBABLY BEEN EXPOSED TO *RADIATION*!"

"I'M GUESSING IT'S SUCKING *IN* RADIATION, CHARGING ITS *BATTERIES*, SO TO SPEAK."

"AT LEAST THAT WOULD EXPLAIN..."

"IN ANY CASE, IT MIGHT BE *SAFER* TO SEE FROM A *DISTANCE*!"

WHUNK

"...THE *LOOK* OF THIS PLACE AND POOR *FLORENSKY'S* SKULL.*"

*LAST ISSUE.

NO MORE GAS-- LUCKY IT WORKED AT ALL.

GOOD THING OUR FRIENDS HAD MORE PRESSING MATTERS. WHAT ARE THOSE CLOUDS?

NITROUS OXYGEN, THEY'RE TRYING TO FREEZE IT. IT'S PROBABLY HOW THEY GOT IT HERE IN THE FIRST PLACE.

HOW'S THE OLD MAN?

APRIL 17
WHITE SANDS VALLEY
10:06 A.M.

NOT VERY GOOD, HE CAN'T WALK.

I WISH AT LEAST WE KNEW WHAT HE WAS SAYING.

⟨BROTHER FOX WOULD NOT LET US DIE.⟩

MAYBE HE'S IN SHOCK-- SPEAKING SOME NATIVE AMERICAN DIALECT. I HAVEN'T THE FOGGIEST IDEA WHAT HE WAS SAYING.

STAY WITH HIM, I'LL TRY TO FIND SOME HELP.

AT TIMES, WITH MY HEART IN MY THROAT, I WANT TO DROP EVEN THE PRETENSE OF ARGUMENT. I WANT TO SAY, MULDER, YOU'RE ABSOLUTELY RIGHT.

THE WORLD CAN CAVE IN AT ANY GIVEN MOMENT. EVERYTHING REALLY IS ALWAYS UP FOR GRABS.

THE ALIENS ARE COMING! OYSTERS ARE TAKING OVER THE WORLD! HOW COULD I HAVE BEEN SO BLIND?

BUT OF COURSE, BEFORE I CAN SAY ANYTHING, HE'S GONE.

<HE REACHES OUT AND PLUCKS THE FRUIT.>

NO, SIR, I...

<BUT THE TASTE IS ALWAYS BITTER.>

<HE LONGS TO REST, BUT CANNOT FIND HIS HOME.>

<I PRAY THAT YOU HELP HIM, NOT FOR HIS SAKE, BUT FOR YOUR OWN.>

<OR, IN HIS BLINDNESS, HE MAY CONSUME THE EARTH...>

LAS CRUCES
28 MILES

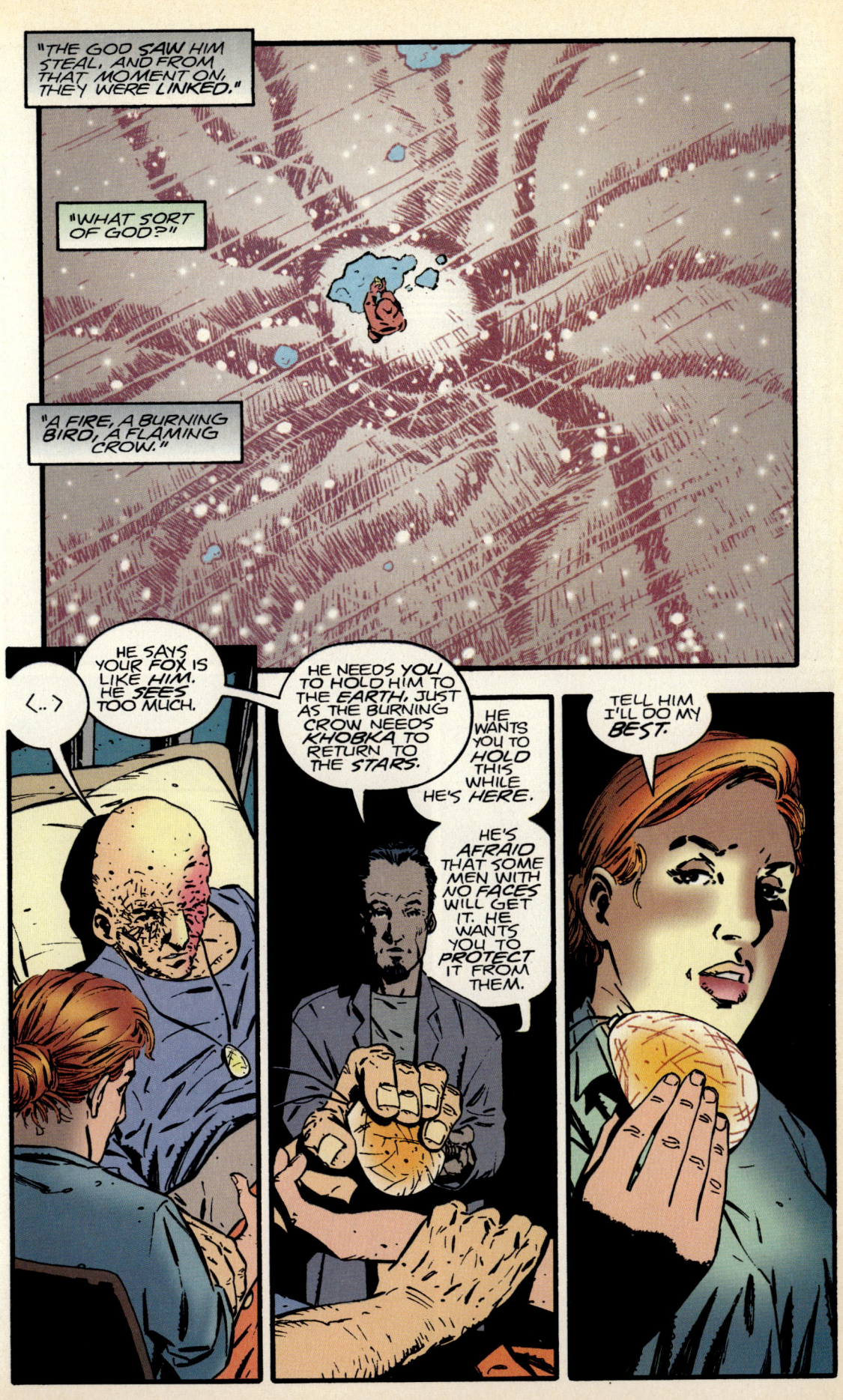

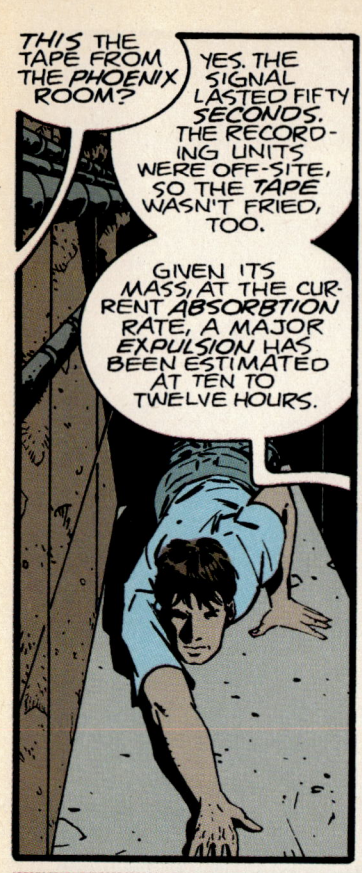

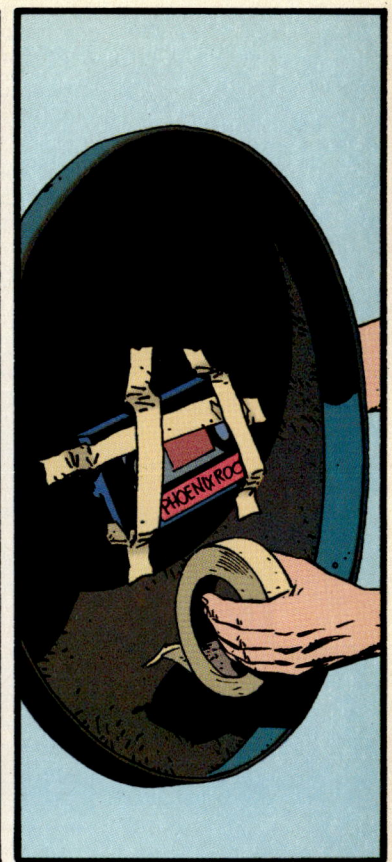

"IT'S FEEDING ON ALL *SORTS* OF ENERGY."

"IT'S ONLY A MATTER OF TIME BEFORE IT REACHES ITS MAXIMUM CAPACITY. IF IT BLOWS, *MILLIONS* OF AMERICANS WILL DIE."

"THEN WHY DID YOU BRING IT HERE IN THE FIRST PLACE?"

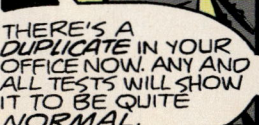
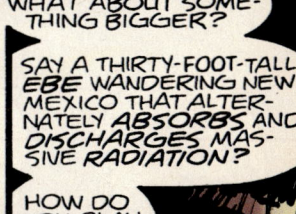

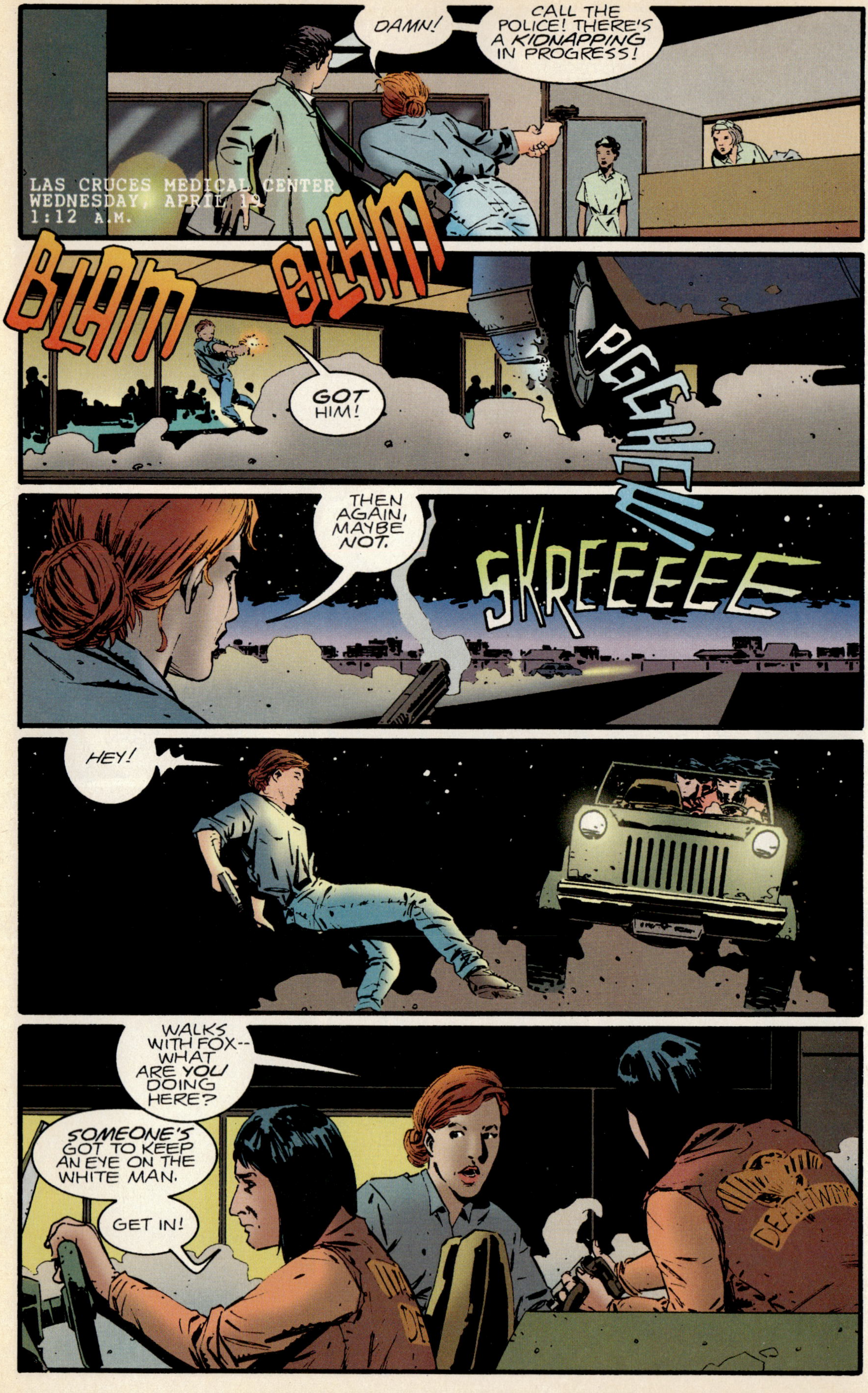

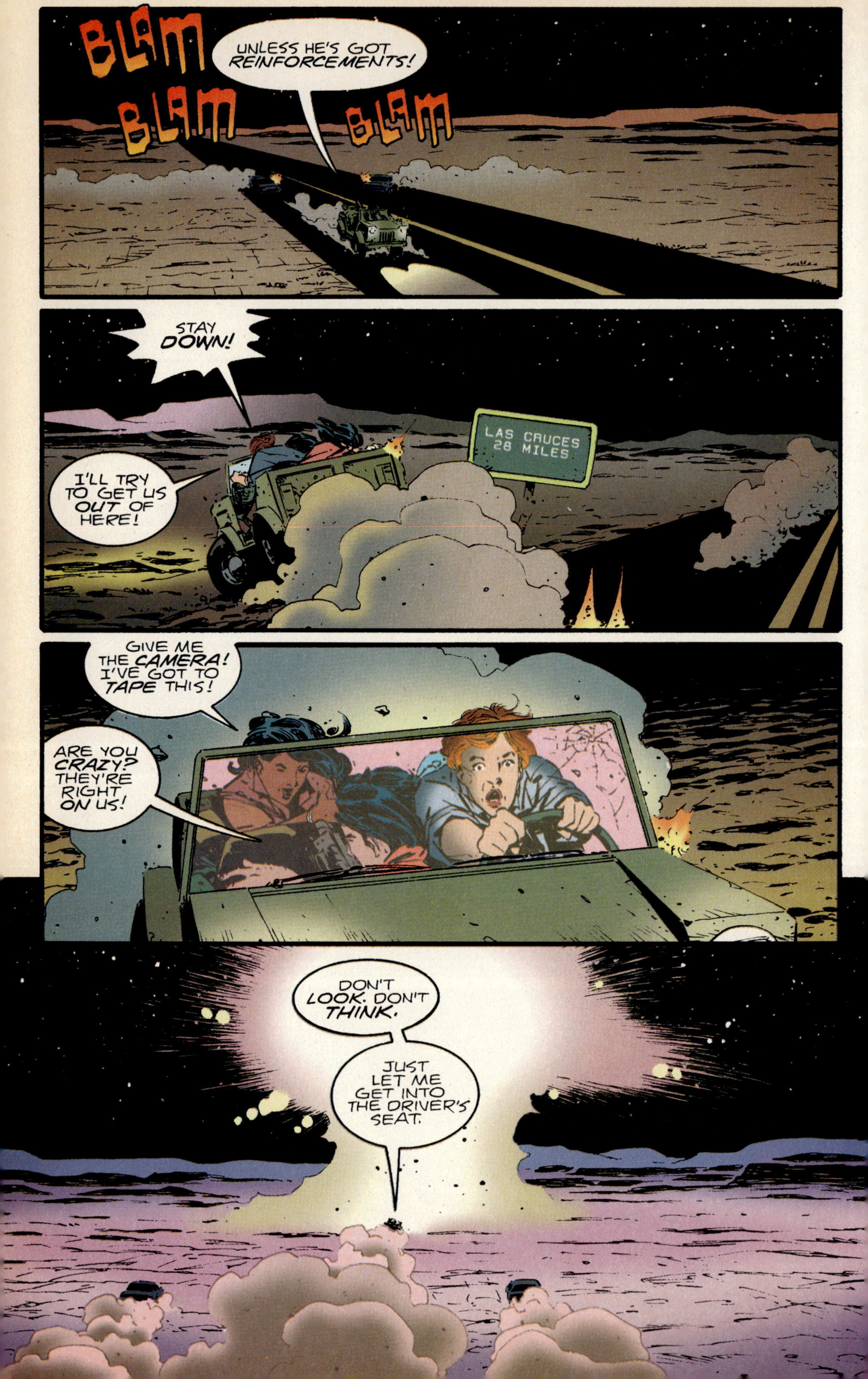

PHOENIX SIGHTED, GENERAL SHADENFREUD.

DAMN *SCIENTISTS* THOUGHT THEY HAD IT *ALL* FIGURED OUT.

NEVER EVEN *GUESSED* THAT ONCE IT ABSORBED ENOUGH ENERGY, THEY'D *NEVER* BE ABLE TO CONTAIN IT.

PHOENIX IS ALMOST IN *RANGE*, SIR.

GLAD TO HEAR IT, SOLDIER.

I WAS GETTING *BORED.*

KAROOOM

"ARE YOU SURE?"

"IT'S TAKEN IN ALL THE ENERGY IT CAN. IT'S GOING TO BLOW."

"KHOBKA BELIEVES IT NEEDS THAT CRYSTAL TO CONTROL ITSELF-- AND ONLY HE CAN GIVE IT TO HIM."

"WE STOPPED HIM LAST TIME."

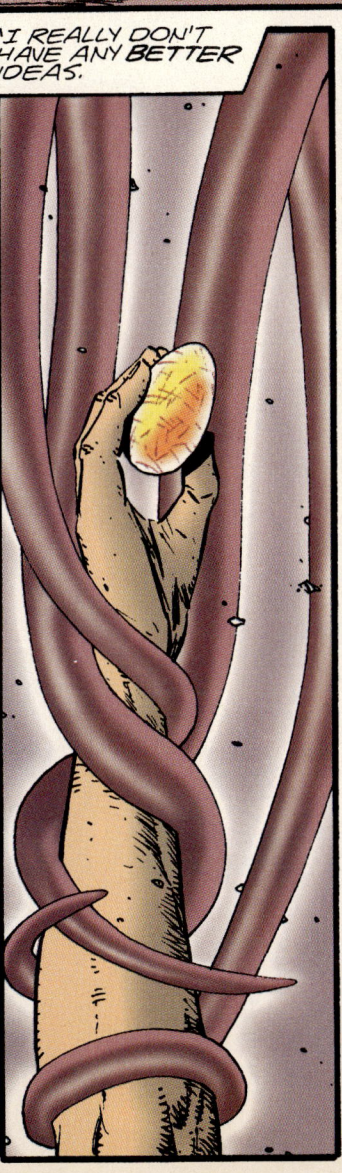
"I REALLY DON'T HAVE ANY BETTER IDEAS."

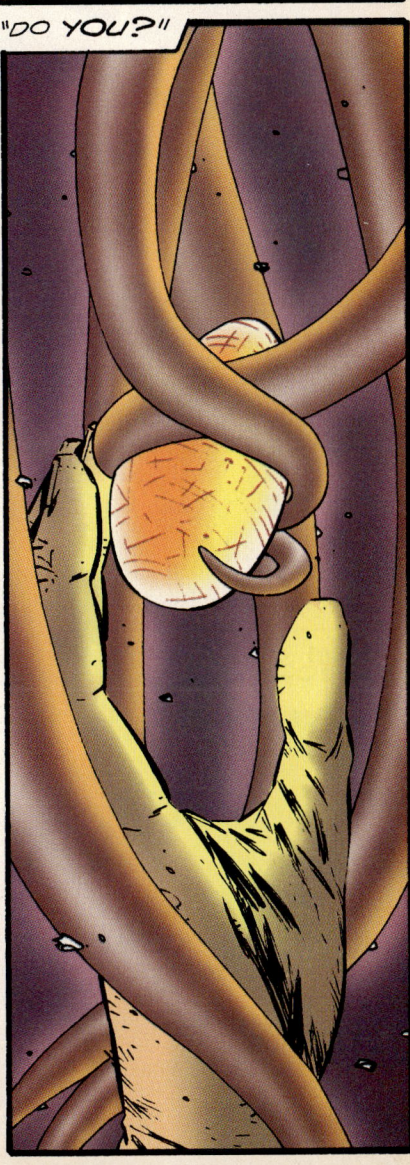
"DO YOU?"

MARCH 5, 1995
TULSA, OKLAHOMA
2 A.M.

AHHHHH!

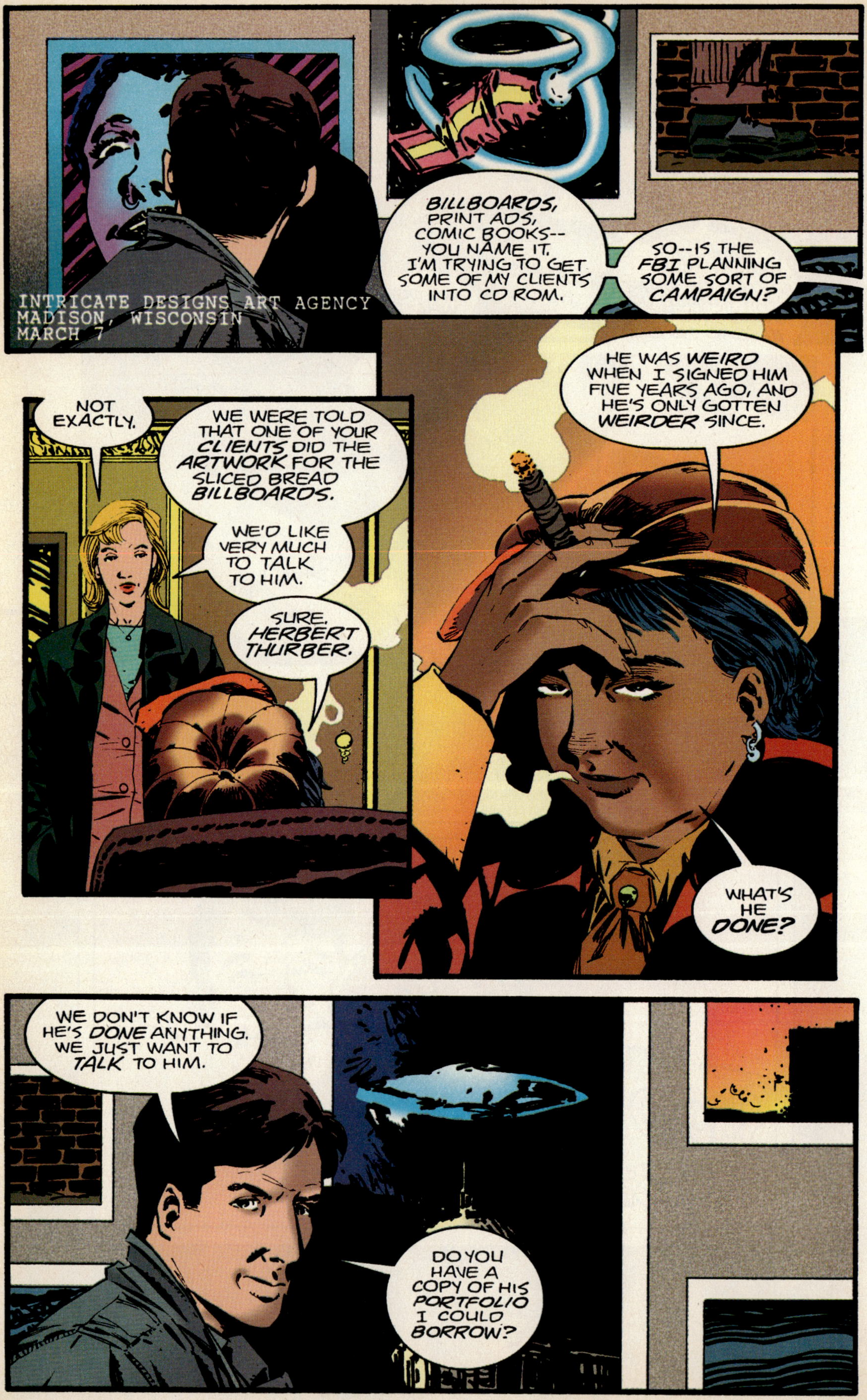

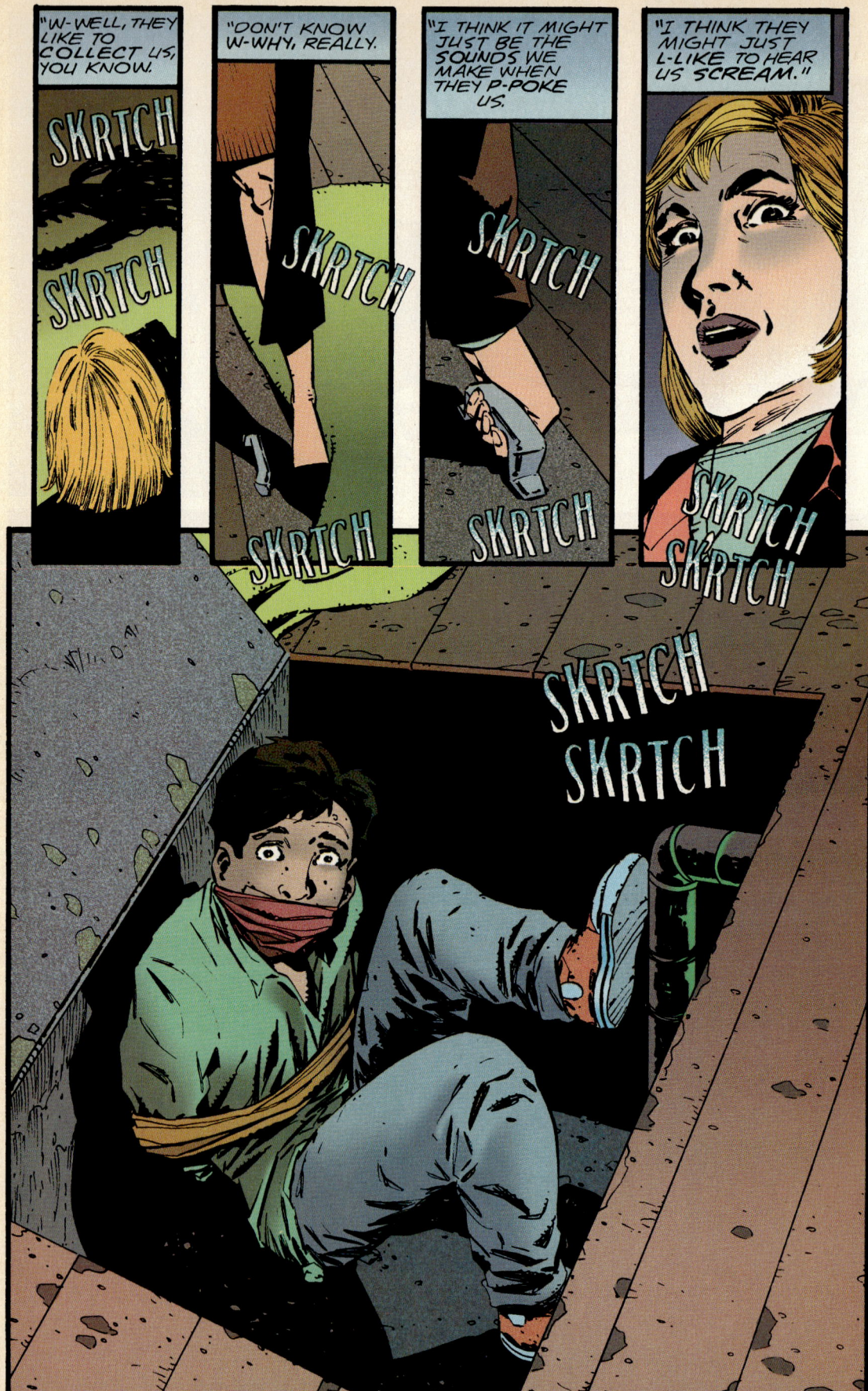

MARCH 10, 1995
ST. PAUL CORRECTIONAL FACILITY
2 A.M.

MIRAN KIM

X-FILES cover artist Miran Kim is a Korean-American who was born in Newark, New Jersey, in 1968 and raised in Seoul, Korea. Miran has achieved the distinction of being a rising star in both the popular culture and the fine art worlds. Miran illustrated a comic book story for the recently released hardcover anthology WEIRD BUSINESS edited by Joe R. Lansdale and Richard Klaw. For Topps Miran did trading card illustrations for STAR WARS GALAXY Series 2 and MARS ATTACKS. Miran was the cover artist on Marvel's HELLRAISER and Vertigo's ANIMAL MAN series. In addition Miran has done horror and romance covers for the paperback publisher Zebra. She is especially proud of her collaboration with the horror writer Poppy Z. Brite on the project "Becoming The Monster." Miran has also worked on the Public Enemy music video "Shut 'em Down." Equally important to her is the fact that she has had a number of fine art shows, both solo and group, many with a socio-political edge. The most famous of these shows is Chongsin Dae or "Comfort Women," the name specific to young Korean women sexually enslaved in military brothels for the entertainment of Japanese soldiers during World War II. This show was presented at the Korean Embassy in New York City and is presently being featured at the NGO Forum on Women in Beijing, China.

STEFAN PETRUCHA

PHOTOS: CHARLES S. NOVINSKIE/TOPPS COMICS

In his ten years as a professional writer, Stefan Petrucha has done everything from comics to tech writing to assisting legendary writer/director Joseph L. Mankiewicz. Starting with SQUALOR, which one reviewer called a "rattling kick-along through quantum mechanics and astral projection" Stefan, who was born in The Bronx in 1959, established a reputation for having an eclectic style grounded in popular genres and often tinged with a bizarre touch of humor. For First Comics Stefan created the superhero team series META-4 which dealt with crystal healing, tantric magic, the history of UFOs and many other aspects of the paranormal phenomena which he would later use in THE X-FILES comic book series. No stranger to the superhero world, Stefan has also written NEXUS THE LIBERATOR for Dark Horse and a recent WHAT IF—? for Marvel Comics.

On the satirical side, Stefan created LANCE BARNES: POST NUKE DICK for Marvel's Epic line and COUNTERPARTS for Tundra Publishing. And Stefan was the writer of Topps Comics' DUCKMAN title, based on the critically acclaimed animation series on the USA Network.

After watching the first episodes of THE X-FILES television series, Stefan fell in love with the show and approached Topps Comics with the idea of doing the comic book adaptation. Stefan is now happy scripting both the monthly X-FILES comic book series and the X-FILES COMICS DIGEST. Stefan and his wife Sarah are expecting their first child in September.

CHARLES ADLARD

X-FILES interior artist Charles Adlard has won the praise of X-Philes for the way his dark, moody, naturalistic style captures the feel and spirit of the television show. Born in England in 1966, Charles's professional debut occurred in 1991 in Fleetway's JUDGE DREDD magazine. From there he worked for Marvel UK, doing DANCES WITH DEMONS. This was followed by assignments for Defiant, DC and Marvel. Charles's first major comic book project was Topps Comics' MARS ATTACKS series which debuted in 1994. In that series, Charles depicted scenes ranging from military conferences and attacks, to jungle encounters with giant insects, to terrifying confrontations between hospital staff members, Martian Death Squad troopers and giant cockroaches. Charles is presently doing the artwork for the new MARS ATTACKS: COUNTERSTRIKE series. In addition he did the artwork for the recently released SUPREME ANNUAL for Image, and was the inker on the "Lunatik" serial for MARVEL COMICS PRESENTS.

TRUST NO ONE